W9-CUY-762

The Red Tent

BARNES & NOBLE® READER'S COMPANION™
Today's take on tomorrow's classics.

FICTION
THE CORRECTIONS by Jonathan Franzen
I KNOW WHY THE CAGED BIRD SINGS by Maya Angelou
THE JOY LUCK CLUB by Amy Tan
THE LOVELY BONES by Alice Sebold
THE POISONWOOD BIBLE by Barbara Kingsolver
THE RED TENT by Anita Diamant
WE WERE THE MULVANEYS by Joyce Carol Oates
WHITE TEETH by Zadie Smith

NONFICTION
THE ART OF WAR by Sun Tzu
A BRIEF HISTORY OF TIME by Stephen Hawking
GUNS, GERMS, AND STEEL by Jared Diamond
JOHN ADAMS by David McCullough

ANITA DIAMANT'S

The Red Tent

BARNES
&NOBLE
BOOKS

EDITORIAL DIRECTOR Justin Kestler
EXECUTIVE EDITOR Ben Florman
DIRECTOR OF TECHNOLOGY Tammy Hepps

SERIES EDITOR John Crowther
MANAGING EDITOR Vincent Janoski

WRITER Lois Ruby
EDITOR Matt Blanchard
DESIGN Dan O. Williams, Matt Daniels

This edition published by Spark Publishing

Spark Publishing
A Division of SparkNotes LLC
120 Fifth Avenue, 8th Floor
New York, NY 10011

ISBN 1-58663-860-2

Library of Congress Cataloging-in-Publication Data available upon request

Printed and bound in the United States

Contents

BARNES & NOBLE® READER'S COMPANION™

WITH INTELLIGENT CONVERSATION AND ENGAGING commentary from a variety of perspectives, BARNES & NOBLE READER'S COMPANIONS are the perfect complement to today's most widely read and discussed books.

○ ○ ○

Whether you're reading on your own or as part of a book club, BARNES & NOBLE READER'S COMPANIONS provide insights and perspectives on today's most interesting reads: What are other people saying about this book? What's the author trying to tell me?

○ ○ ○

Pick up the BARNES & NOBLE READER'S COMPANION to learn more about what you're reading. From the big picture down to the details, you'll get today's take on tomorrow's classics.

The Red Tent

The Greatest Story Ever Retold

The Red Tent tells the story of Jacob and his family from a whole new perspective—that of the women.

THE BIBLE IS FULL OF VOICES. From the unnamed narrator of the creation story of Genesis to the Hebrew prophets to the haunting poet of the Song of Solomon, the Bible gives us a wealth of perspectives from ancient times.

But some voices are missing. For each of the unforgettable biblical figures we remember today, there are many who have slipped silently through the cracks of history. We know precious little about them, about who they were, about their place in the biblical world.

Among these silenced voices is Dinah. The eleventh child and only daughter of Jacob, Dinah is consigned to the smallest of roles in the Bible. We see her name just a few times, scattered across several later chapters of Genesis. Almost every time, Dinah's name is paired with disturbing images and pictures of violence. All we know of her is that a prince of Shechem rapes her and that her brothers, after demanding the "bride price" of circumcision for every male in Shechem, exact an unthinkable revenge—the murder of every male in Shechem.

After this massacre, we never hear of Dinah again. Even her own father neglects to mention her on his deathbed while he curses and blesses his other children. Today, if we speak of her at all, we usually mispronounce her name as Dye-nah rather than the correct Dee-nah.

The Red Tent

Anita Diamant's novel *The Red Tent* changes everything. Suddenly, Dinah blossoms into a full character—in fact, the narrator and main character of a story all her own. Diamant opens a window into the everyday lives of Dinah and her female counterparts from the Bible. In the red tent of the novel's title, we watch as the young Dinah witnesses all the rituals of womanhood. As she and her biblical mothers celebrate the synchronization of their cycles with the rhythms of the moon, they nibble sweets, murmur stories and secrets, and share days of rest from their grueling toil under the sun. This tent is also the place where each woman labors to deliver new life, where each baby draws its first breath—or none. Dinah is the only girl who sits among the women.

The Red Tent salvages Dinah's name and image, weaving from the barest of threads a tapestry of tragedy and triumph, of common life spent beneath the primitive pull of the moon, and of high life pulsing with palace intrigue. Although Diamant's version of the story is different from the biblical version, *The Red Tent* remains believable because Diamant embellishes it with details about history and geography, religion and superstition, food, dress, lodging, family rituals, manners, and the medical practices of a gritty life lived in tents among flocks of goats and sheep.

Told in the first person, Dinah's tale unfolds in three books: "My Mothers' Stories," "My Story," and "Egypt." The first two expand on what we know of her family and daily life from the scant biblical passages that concern Dinah—but the third book, "Egypt," is complete fiction. Much of it rings true in the well-researched customs of the household of a rich, powerful Egyptian family. Diamant gives us a what-if—the future Dinah might have faced after the violence in Shechem that left her a young widow drenched in the blood of her beloved. In Egypt, Dinah becomes many things: a lonely soul with idle hands used to spinning wool; a mother who must share her son with another woman and hide his past from him; a foreign midwife respected in Egyptian cities; a friend; an embittered sister and daughter; and finally, a contented wife. This final section of the novel rings with reality and yet it's pure storytelling—storytelling that compels us not to forget Dinah as others have forgotten her before.

PROLOGUE

Voiceless for 3,500 years, Dinah now speaks to us directly: "My name means nothing to you. My memory is dust." So begins *The Red Tent*, a provocative twist on a horrifying biblical story. As the sad tone of the prologue hints, Dinah will be a heroine forged in the fires of tragedy, for the lives of women in her day are full of hardship. Conditions are harsh under the sun. The grinding of grain, the cooking, washing, healing, and spinning are endless—except during the new moon, when the women gather in the red tent.

Polygamy is a double-edged sword for these women. It breeds jealousy among the wives of a shared husband while at the same time providing the comfort of sisters and the guarantee of many sons. What the women secretly long for are daughters who will learn their arts, hear their stories, and keep their memories. After ten sons surround their father, Dinah, the only daughter, is born, a long-awaited gift to the women.

PART ONE
MY MOTHERS' STORIES

Near the city of Haran (in the area of present-day Iraq and Syria) live a disreputable, greedy man named Laban and his four daughters. Leah and Rachel are the daughters of Laban's wives, while Bilhah and Zilpah, daughters of his concubines, serve as handmaidens to their higher-ranking sisters.

Leah and Rachel are markedly different from one another. Leah, the eldest, is tall, full-bodied, fearless, and in charge. Her strange eyes are of two different colors and lack eyelashes, so it appears as if she never blinks. Some whisper that Leah should've been drowned at birth, with such eyes. In the Bible, we're told that Leah's eyes are weak, but Dinah says this isn't so. Leah's eyes are so haunting that people avert theirs when they first see her. Jacob, however, doesn't—which is why she falls in love with him immediately.

Rachel, on the other hand, is beautiful and petite, with golden skin, bronze hair and obsidian-black eyes. Her disposition doesn't fit her lovely appearance. She's petulant and selfish and feels quite deserving when

Jacob, a stranger (although her cousin) encounters her at a well and kisses her full on the mouth. The two pledge to marry, and Jacob gives Rachel a blue lapis ring as a betrothal gift.

This ring is a significant token that comes full circle at the end of *The Red Tent*, when Dinah's brother, Judah, gives her the ring at the time of their father's death. Curiously, it's not Rachel but one of the mothers who initially entrusts the ring to Judah. It's Leah who asks her son to give this ring to Dinah as a symbol that Leah at last has come to peace in her life-long rivalry with her sister Rachel. We might assume that Rachel, her life slipping away as she gives birth to Benjamin, bequeaths the ring to Leah as a token of reconciliation. Leah clings to the hope that Dinah won't be lost to her forever, so she holds the ring for her daughter to remind Dinah that forgiveness mends a fragmented heart.

The original significance of the lapis ring is Jacob's promise to Rachel that they will marry as soon as possible. But Rachel is "unripe"—she hasn't yet begun to have her menstrual periods—so the wedding is postponed. Meanwhile, negotiations go on between Jacob, who must offer a bride price, and Laban, who is duty-bound to provide a dowry. The bride price is steep: seven months of Jacob's labor. This detail is one of many instances in which Diamant diverges from the biblical account, which says that Jacob labors for seven *years*, not seven months.

But when Jacob unveils his bride, he finds Leah, rather than his beloved Rachel, in his bed. Still, he takes Leah as his wife and finds pleasure in her—but then has to pledge Laban another seven months of labor to win Rachel. We sense from the start that this two-wife arrangement will doom the sisters to a lifetime of jealousy. And indeed it does cause great jealousy—which only grows worse later, when Bilhah and Zilpah are sent to Jacob's tent as surrogates to produce sons for their mistresses.

No more surprises

Traditional Jewish weddings include a ceremony directly before the nuptials during which the groom unveils the bride in front of the guests. No one expects the bride to be switched with her sister these days, nor does anyone believe that a discerning groom could be so easily fooled. Nevertheless, this ritual survives some 3,500 years since the trickery that disappointed Jacob on his wedding day.

We can only imagine the complications of four wives and nothing but goatskin walls to muffle the stirrings.

The red tent of the title is a bustling place where all the women of the extended family gather as their menstrual cycles coincide with the new moon. Such synchronicity might seem strange, but research has indeed shown that women who live in close community, especially tribal women who live exposed to the moon, usually synchronize their cycles. Regardless, Diamant's concern is in the realm of biblical literature, not science. The premise of the monthly gatherings in the red tent establishes a secret, hidden women's world, where the mysteries and ceremonies of womanhood unfold as girls come of age and babies wail their way into the world.

Leah bears six sons—an achievement that doesn't endear her to Rachel, who appears to be barren. To compensate, Rachel learns the art of midwifery, one of the few professional skills open to women at the time. A midwife not only assisted in births but also learned the secrets of herbs and healing balms. She would have freedom to venture away to attend to laboring mothers in other camps.

Thus, the stage is set for Dinah, still only a dream, to follow in Rachel's footsteps years later. With the passing seasons, Jacob turns Laban into a wealthy man, even as his own flock increases—both in terms of livestock and in sons, which number ten. Finally, after all four mothers foretell her birth in their dreams, a girl is born. Dinah's birth bathes the women with such joy and relief that Rachel finally conceives Joseph, who becomes Dinah's milk-brother and childhood companion. Many years, many heartaches later, their lives will chillingly dovetail, a world away from the red tent of their mothers.

PART TWO
MY STORY

This section plunges us into the dramatic core of the novel, as Dinah grows from carefree child to midwife's apprentice, ultimately becoming the cause of the terrible bloodshed that defines her adult life. She matures before our eyes, and through *her* eyes we see those events that shape her future. The growing differences among the four mothers become clear, as does the contrast between their pagan rituals and the One God of Jacob. Meanwhile, Dinah realizes that her mothers are subtly powerful. And when Dinah's father, Jacob, prepares to lead the family back to the land of his birth after he has served twenty years as an underling to the loathsome Laban, Dinah recognizes her father as a handsome man, worthy of a creature as wondrous as her mother, Leah.

Jacob and his family's journey is quite an undertaking: thirty people on foot, carrying household goods, treasures, and babies. Oxcarts bear tents and looms, dogs herd restless flocks of goats and sheep across desert land and dangerous rivers. It's in the preparations for this journey that Dinah observes the abiding love between her mother and father, as well as the craftiness of Rachel, who steals Laban's household idols to protect them on their journey.

In a **riveting moment,** Rebecca peers into Dinah's face and **foretells** a **great sorrow awaiting** her.

The wandering tribe encounters dangers and surprises, among them two women who become minor but key characters in *The Red Tent*. One is Inna, the midwife who teaches Rachel her skills. The other is Werenro, an exotic redhead who leads the travelers to the grandmother, Rebecca. For Jacob, the journey is a terrifying one, as he anticipates his encounter with his elder brother, Esau. From biblical history, we know that a lifetime earlier, the brothers parted angrily after Rebecca conspired with Jacob to steal Esau's birthright.

We recall the famous biblical account of Jacob wrestling with the angel when we read that Jacob, wracked with guilt and dread, undergoes a transforming experience that leaves him battered and emotionally confused. Joseph, who finds Jacob in this state, is also changed—as any son might be when learning that his father is not invincible.

The reunion with Esau and his horde is almost an anticlimax, as the brothers fall into each other's arms and their families embrace. Dinah is eager to meet grandmother, but Rebecca isn't what Dinah expected. Known as the Oracle, she's imperious and impatient, robed in purple, perfumed and vain. Rebecca is unkind to her family even as she rains kindness upon strangers. Dinah despises her, all the more so when

Rebecca demands that Dinah stay behind after her family continues on its journey. The reasons for Rebecca's request are unclear, but they may range from pure contrariness on Rebecca's part to Rebecca's recognition of a special spirit in Dinah that needs seasoning under Rebecca's tutelage.

Whatever the reason, Dinah remains in her grandmother's tent, longing for the company of her mothers. She never learns to love Rebecca, but she does come to honor Rebecca for her deeds as oracle. In a riveting moment, Rebecca peers into Dinah's face and foretells a great sorrow awaiting her. This ominous cloud hangs over Dinah's head for the three months she dwells in Rebecca's tent and long after Dinah returns to her family, when her work as Rachel's apprentice leads her into the nearby city of Shechem. The sights and scents of the city and the opulence of the palace enthrall Dinah—as does the beauty of the prince, named Shalem in this novel. At this point, the story becomes a heart-racing drama that catapults us to its tragic and bloody climax.

Dinah and Shalem fall passionately in love at that first meeting and become bride and groom in an era when marriages are sealed not by ceremony, but by consummation. The consummation is steamy. Unlike the alleged rapist in the Bible, the Shalem of *The Red Tent* is honorable, and his father offers Jacob a generous bride price that will forge a union and many marriages between the two peoples.

Jacob, often clueless as to what's going on among the women in his family, allows his sons Levi and Simon to convince him that Dinah didn't go to Shalem's arms willingly. But Levi and Simon have their own agenda. Always the mean bullies among the brothers, now they fear that their status will plummet as the political ties between Jacob's family and Shechem rise. Thus Levi and Simon spread the vicious story that Dinah had been forcibly taken—a slander that has far-reaching consequences for both families and from which Dinah never fully recovers.

To restore Dinah's honor, Jacob's family must seek revenge—Jacob demands as bride price that all the males of Shechem be circumcised in the manner of his own people. While this demand seems outrageous to the modern mind, we must remember that more marriages than Dinah's are at stake, and that at the time it was unthinkable for Jacob's women to consort with men who hadn't been circumcised. Still, it's a dreadful bargain, but one that Shalem and Hamor willingly accept.

Their unfortunate subjects have no choice but to go under the knife as well. The suffering is immense.

If that were the end of the matter, in three days the men would be healed, Dinah and Shalem would live happily ever after, and *The Red Tent* would end on page 200. But bloodlust still rages in Levi and Simon. So while the men of Shechem recover from their ordeal, the brothers slaughter all of them, including Dinah's beloved husband. They drag their sister off to her father's camp.

Where is Jacob in all this bloody chaos? *The Red Tent* remains silent on that question, but Dinah does not. In her overwhelming grief and rage, she curses her father, spits in his face, declares him dead to her, and returns to Shechem. Concluding this section of the novel, Dinah muses on how her life might have turned out differently if her kinder brother, Reuben, had pulled her back to her family. She would have lived out her life bitter and dead to the core—were it not for the fact that the gods had another fate awaiting her in Egypt.

PART THREE
EGYPT

The life Dinah leads among her husband's family in Egypt is strangely hollow. She agonizes through nightmares of the bloody events in her recent past, but her mother-in-law refuses to speak of her dead son, Shalem. We sense that the people of the palace tolerate Dinah—now called by her Egyptian name, Den-ner—only because of the unborn heir she carries. We sense that when the boy is born and weaned, Dinah will lose her status.

More skilled than the midwives who serve the palace, Dinah all but delivers her own child in rituals far less comforting than those she has known among her own people. It's fascinating to compare the birthing practices across the two cultures—those of Egypt appear impersonal and emotionally sterile compared to the advanced midwifery techniques and female communal support practiced in the Israelite culture.

Dinah's joy at the birth of Bar Shalem, "son of Shalem," flags when she's told that his name is to be changed to Re-mose—and that officially he's her mother-in-law's child, to replace the murdered son. A prophecy fills Dinah with both pride and dread: Re-mose will someday be a great prince of Egypt. Dinah revels in Re-mose's every smile and antic for nine years, until he is cruelly removed from her to study in a distant city so as to prepare for his lofty future.

Now childless, Dinah feels invisible in the palace. Desperate for something useful to do, she begins to attend the births of Egyptian women. Her growing reputation calls her to the great houses in Thebes. In gratitude for her aid in delivering healthy babies to mothers who actually survive—many did not in those days—Dinah receives scores of trinkets as gifts, enough to fill a beautiful chest carved by the master carpenter, Benia. The gentle Benia causes Dinah's heart to thunder, her eyes to brighten for the first time in years, rekindling the hope for love. And yet, Dinah wonders, does she dare give her heart again, when she considers her soul dead?

A chance encounter with Werenro, Rebecca's fiery messenger from many years back, reminds Dinah that she is in fact *alive*, that the flame of love still burns strongly within her. Dinah has been harboring hate all through her adult life. Love and hate are often tied together, though, so

"Of all life's pleasures, only love owes no debt to death."

it's no surprise to find that love dwells in Dinah's heart behind the shield of hate. Bravely, Dinah marries Benia and, for the first time in her life, nests in a home of her own.

Re-mose, meanwhile, has grown into an arrogant man, nearly a stranger to his mother. He serves as scribe to a powerful vizier, a Canaanite known as Zaphenat-Paneh-ah, whom the Egyptian king favors. If we read carefully and have familiarity with the bible, we quickly guess that this Zaphenat must be none other than Dinah's brother, Joseph, who calls for the Canaanite midwife to assist in delivering his first son.

Diamant has to convey a great deal of information in a short span to expose this link between Dinah and Joseph. To accelerate the connection, she provides us with a gossiping slave woman who sits beside Dinah's sickbed, recounting the story of Joseph's rise from prisoner in the king's dungeon to near-prince. Hearing the story, Dinah recognizes the dramatic turns of her own brother's life. But her reunion with Joseph isn't sweet, for she still blames all her brothers for the terrible bloodshed in Shechem.

What's more, Re-mose finally learns about the death of his father and Zaphenat-Paneh-ah's guilt by association. He threatens the life of Joseph, the vizier—a capital offense. Only through Dinah's pleading is Re-mose spared. But she pays a heavy price for this boldness: Re-mose is banished to a remote corner of Egypt, so Dinah and her son will never meet again.

We can't say the same for Dinah and Joseph. As life ebbs away from their father, Jacob, the brother and sister are summoned to his deathbed. All the mothers already lie in graves when Joseph returns as a favored son. Aside from Judah, none of Dinah's kin recognize her after some thirty years, nor does she reveal herself. So, in a clever plot device, Diamant reveals the family's history over the years through the girlish prattling of a niece.

This portion of *The Red Tent* raises an essential question—whether Dinah is truly forgotten. By all indications, she is. When Jacob blesses his children in his last breath, Dinah listens for her name, but it's never spoken. Saddened, she returns to Thebes and to Benia, to live out her days in quiet contentment, with the images of her four mothers dancing in the dreams of her final nights on earth.

In the final pages of the novel, Diamant takes poetic license in the narrative point of view—we learn much through Dinah's eyes after her own death. Dinah explains this bizarre twist by saying, "I died but I did not leave them." She goes on to say that her memory lingers with Benia until his death, that a niece names her daughter Dinah, and that Re-mose goes on to have children and grandchildren. Dinah concludes by conjuring the image of the lotus flower, which, according to the Egyptians, never dies. And so it is with Dinah, one who is loved and therefore remembered always.

Dinah and Her Sisters

The names are familiar to us, but the personalities aren't. What makes the women of *The Red Tent* different from their biblical counterparts?

IF *THE RED TENT* WERE AN ORDINARY biblical family saga, Jacob, the patriarch, would be the star. But Diamant's novel focuses on the power of women, leaving the men as shadowy figures. Just like the movie trick when the cameras shift one character into clear focus and leave the others fuzzy in the background, Diamant makes sure that we *only* see the women sharply, and that we see the men *only* through the women's eyes—mostly Dinah's.

Diamant has a vision for Dinah and the other women in her novel. She strives to portray them not as victims but as active agents in their own lives. But we can't control when we're born, or who our family will be. Psychologists might say that we love most what we can't have. Four mothers produce son after son, all the while longing for a daughter to carry on their legacy. When she's born, finally, each of the mothers invests her love and unique talents in the one female child among them. The sheltered Dinah feels adored—and *entitled* to that adoration.

DINAH: ADORED AND CURSED

No wonder Dinah's stunned when her grandmother, Rebecca, doesn't acknowledge her as special, despite her status as the only daughter in Jacob's family. This is Dinah's first clue, at perhaps age eleven, that her life isn't golden. In fact, Rebecca predicts great unhappiness for Dinah, and that sorrow unfurls through the rest of the novel. Dinah, having been promised so much in the warmth and security of the red tent, now must feel that the gods are cruel—and she hasn't even begun to speculate on the justice of her father's God. Dinah is a mere child when the red tent is folded and laid upon an oxcart as Jacob leads the family away from the only home she has ever known. After so long in the desert, her first encounter with river water is exhilarating. Inna, the midwife, tells Dinah that she's a child of water, that only by a river will she be happy. By the end of *The Red Tent*, that prediction turns out to be true.

Dinah makes startling discoveries on the journey to Canaan. She sees that fire burns between her parents, that Jacob—not she herself—is first in her mother's heart. Dinah also observes that her all-powerful father is plagued with fear and indecision over the reunion with his brother, that

> ## "My name means nothing to you. My memory is dust."

his body is battered by an encounter with a mysterious adversary. All the anchors in Dinah's life—home, adoration, her father's omnipotence—are pulled from beneath her. New dangers alert Dinah to her mother's warning that "life costs blood."

Dinah's coming-of-age ceremony, in the red tent under the dark of the moon, reels with celebration, with wild and primitive ritual. It would be interesting to know about male puberty rites at the same time, but this topic isn't within Diamant's scope. And what greater power do women have than to bring forth life? How alluring the vocation of midwifery must be to Dinah, doubling her potential power.

Yet this portal into the lives of laboring women leads to the central tragedy of Dinah's own life, as she's called to the palace in Shechem. The rest, as they say, is history: the love affair (or is it rape?), the slaughter of the males in Shechem, and Dinah's rejection of her family to join her mother-in-law in Egypt. We must look critically at the romance Diamant invents. Would a sheltered girl of Dinah's upbringing leave everything to plunge into a sexual relationship with a man of a different culture and social status? Maybe the hunger for that sort of love is great enough to make such a choice believable. What *is* entirely believable is that Dinah has no choice but to leave her family after the horrendous violence that her brothers commit and that her father does not condemn. Returning to Shechem and going on to Egypt are Dinah's only options if she's to survive emotionally.

In the Egyptian palace, Dinah feels a dulling of her senses—or rather a telescoping of her senses inward upon the life she carries. Everything changes at Bar Shalem's birth. Dinah is ecstatic as she names the boy for his father, and in the next moment, bereft to learn that she's to be marginal in the infant's life, barely more than a wet nurse. How different from the love Dinah's four mothers showered upon her when she nestled in the very center of their lives. Dinah is suddenly adrift, far from her own people. Yet destiny tugs her to the inevitable rendezvous with Joseph.

Dinah draws upon her native talent for midwifery and the skills she's gleaned from the two cultures in which she's lived, and in due time she's called upon to attend the birth of Joseph's son. The similarity between this summons and the one that led Dinah to Shechem is clear, and we hold our breath waiting to see if the consequences will be as tragic and life-changing. They're certainly potent enough to propel Dinah toward the novel's second climax, Jacob's death (The first, of course, is the massacre at Shechem). Now a woman past her childbearing years, Dinah comes full circle, to the tents of her childhood.

Indeed, we see many times how Dinah drifts with the current. (It's significant that she only learns to swim at the end of the novel.) From our modern-day perspective, Dinah's passivity comes across as puzzling. At her son's birth, for example, she barely blinks when her mother-in-law renames the boy and claims him as her own son. We almost want to scream out to Dinah to speak up, to fight for once, against getting swept up in the rolling tide of events. But we must put ourselves in her shoes: what incentive does she have to assert herself? The only brazen move Dinah has made—going to Shalem's bed—has turned to overwhelming grief. She doesn't dare risk so much again. Alas, to our great relief, Dinah eventually takes some risks and speaks up at three very significant points in the novel.

The first time Dinah asserts herself, she curses Jacob for his implication in the slaughter at Shechem. The second instance occurs after Re-mose, now a grown man, summons Dinah to deliver his master's son. Thinking only of his career, Re-mose commands her to come at once, but she scolds him soundly until he falls at her feet in shame. It's gratifying to see Dinah at last acting like a mother, teaching her haughty son a thing or two. Dinah's third assertion is her riskiest of all. After Re-mose threatens to kill Joseph—an effrontery for which he must be put to death—Dinah audaciously demands an audience with Joseph to plead for her son's life. Joseph, whether out of shame or sympathy for Dinah's earnest plea, spares Re-mose's life. So Dinah triumphs, but at enormous cost. She will never see her son again.

Dinah stands at crucial intersections many times in the novel, and her choices are sometimes puzzling. She follows her heart and goes to Shalem's bed—but again, look at the price. The decision to marry Benia ends Dinah's loneliness and gives her some peace in her later years, but it also ties her even tighter to Egyptian culture. As much as we might sentimentalize homecomings, Dinah can never go home again. Just as she's been written out of our memory these 3,500 years, so is she stricken from her father's heart—and from her family history, now that all her mothers are gone. Dinah returns to the family at Jacob's death so much a stranger that no one recognizes her.

Why doesn't Joseph introduce her? We may interpret this oversight in different ways. It could be a flaw in the novel, or a technique Diamant uses to preserve the narrative flow. It could be meant to tell us something about Joseph's character, his arrogant, self-centered nature. Or Joseph may mean to protect Dinah from their father as his ultimate act of kindness for his milk-sister. A more likely possibility is that Dinah *chooses* to remain anonymous in order to gather the stories and shield herself from rejection, or from the urging of her niece that she remain among the family. But Jacob's final neglect, his heartless act of omission, seals Dinah's fate, and she returns to Benia to live out her days in a foreign land.

In the melancholy final scenes of the novel, we come to recognize the iron strength in this woman who is able to cast off her bitterness and forgive Joseph, the stand-in for all her brothers. There is tremendous strength in Dinah's fierce determination to be remembered and in the final benediction for those who will learn of her centuries later. The final image Dinah leaves with us is of a self-assured woman who can genuinely look back and see that her life has had purpose, that she has loved—and been loved by—two good men and four remarkable mothers.

REBECCA: THE HEARTLESS MATRIARCH

The most shocking character in *The Red Tent* is, without question, Rebecca. Those of us who grew up with Hebrew scripture are astounded to encounter one of scripture's classic matriarchs portrayed in such a harsh light. We know Rebecca conspired with her favorite son, Jacob, to rob Esau of his birthright, so we're prepared for a woman whose reputation isn't unblemished. But it's disturbing to us that Diamant paints Rebecca as a thoroughly distasteful character. Rebecca is physically vain as she primps with her makeup and perfumes and tosses out silly advice, such as how one's breath should always be sweetened with mint. She's thoughtless to her servants, refusing to see them as individuals.

While those around Rebecca consult and honor her as an oracle and healer, she's curiously cruel to her own family. She emasculates Isaac, her doddering husband, and banishes him to a tent miles away, in the care of one of her servants. Encountering Jacob's wives for the first time, Rebecca grills Leah until the woman sinks in exhaustion, and then Rebecca plainly shows her favoritism for Rachel. But Rebecca prefers even the least of Jacob's wives over Esau's "foreign" wife and her native customs. Thus, Tabea, Rebecca's loving granddaughter, is callously cast away forever, simply because her mother hasn't initiated her into womanhood in the manner Rebecca deems proper. As for Dinah, Rebecca condemns her to three months of loneliness when she demands that Dinah stay behind rather than travel on with her family. No one dares defy such an order.

Diamant must have good reason for twisting the plot, and Dinah's future, in this way. Why does she paint Rebecca as such an unsympathetic character? Does she play loosely with Rebecca's biblical reputation for shock value, to up the stakes and increase the dramatic conflict in *The Red Tent*? Is it because Diamant needs a villain in contrast to Dinah's four romantically drawn mothers, to show that not all women are lovable? Does she mean Rebecca's unsavory character to jar Dinah into reality and toughen her for the grief ahead?

All the above views are valid, but one explanation makes the most sense. If we start with the undeniable premise that *The Red Tent* is a novel about female power, then Rebecca shows us, undeniably, how absolute power corrupts women too.

LEAH: **THE EMBATTLED WIFE**

The least self-centered figure in the novel, Leah is a decision-maker, both a wife and the head of a household. She's "strong and shapely . . . a half head taller than most men," with hips for bearing and the scent of yeast lingering about her. In Dinah's view, Diamant tells us, Leah reeks of "bread and comfort"—but in Jacob's view, Leah reeks of sex. What we see is an earthy, confident woman as much at ease brewing beer and spinning wool as she is in Jacob's bed. Leah agrees to replace her sister as Jacob's bride, on the pretense of sparing Rachel, who's frightened of the demands that Jacob would put upon her in his tent. In truth, the deception thrills Leah. Diamant writes that on their wedding night, when Jacob cries out in pleasure, Leah is flooded with a sense of her own power—nor is Jacob disappointed. Leah wins this skirmish.

Although her father, Laban, is no prize, Leah feels nervous about leaving his home and moving the family to Canaan, as if her confidence will falter in an unfamiliar setting. Yet when all is ready and it's *Jacob* who's apprehensive about taking the first steps on the journey, Leah firmly urges him onward. Leah is clever: she intuitively knows that she must not undermine her husband's authority in the presence of other men, not even her sons. So she softens and flatters Jacob, then coyly asks him if he's ready to dismantle the largest loom and place it on the oxcart. Communication between Leah and Jacob is subtle. He takes the hint and orders their sons to set out on the journey. Another round won for Leah.

As a mother, Leah is loving and efficient, though overrun with quarrelsome sons and impatient with Dinah's handiwork skills. Tenderly, Leah relates the poetry of a girl's coming of age in the traditions of Innana, the great mother goddess. A woman free with words, Leah is speechless with joy when Dinah experiences her first blood. But in the matter of Dinah's romance, Leah's has a more ambiguous stance. She encourages Jacob to allow their daughter to return to Shechem, raising the question of whether Leah, sensitive to Dinah's every mood, knows that her daughter has fallen in love and consciously sends her to the arms of her lover. But when Hamor offers the bride price and speaks crudely of Dinah's sullied virtue, Leah is angry. Is she angry with Dinah for her indiscretion? No. Is she angry with Jacob for allowing Dinah to go back to Shechem? No. Leah is angry with Rachel for initially taking Dinah to attend the birth in the palace. What bubbles to the surface is the old sisterly rivalry between Leah and Rachel more than Leah's concern for her daughter or her horror at the massive violence her sons have wrought.

Throughout the novel, it's Leah to whom Jacob turns for advice and for reports on the welfare of his household. One telling scene comes when the entire family is traveling on foot. Early in the morning, Jacob walks beside Rachel, smiling and enjoying her fresh scent. Later, more seriously, he takes his place beside Leah to talk about the animals and provisions and to seek her advice on etiquette for the upcoming meeting with his parents, Isaac and Rebecca. In short, Jacob loves one wife and relies on the other—and this has to be enough for Leah.

So, with all her competence and cleverness, the Leah of *The Red Tent* is still a tragic, embattled figure. She loves Jacob and has the social advantage of being his first wife. Her fervent hope is that each of the seven sons she gives Jacob will bind him closer to her, but in reality she knows that she'll never be first in his heart. Her sister, Rachel, will always occupy that coveted position.

RACHEL: THE BELOVED WIFE

The novel draws a sharp contrast between Rachel and her sister—Leah is "a mere shadow of Rachel's light." Diamant describes the younger sister as "rare and arresting," smelling like "the scent of fresh water," and with a presence as "powerful as the moon." Rachel is determined that Jacob will be hers, and she wins him in the first few seconds of their meeting. She is conniving, petty and petulant, quick to take and slow to thank. The jealousy between the two sisters flares instantaneously and grows wild as Leah produces son after son in the midst of Rachel's barrenness. To compensate, Rachel becomes a midwife, as if to show her sister that she too can bring life into the world.

What's more, Rachel shapes Dinah, Leah's daughter, into her own image, mentoring her in the techniques and potions used in attending women on the childbirth bricks. The irony is that Rachel, in service to laboring mothers, finds her own tenderness and humanity here, if nowhere else. When finally a pregnancy takes root in Rachel, she nearly dies in delivering Joseph and has no milk for him. Reluctantly, she gives him over to Leah, whose milk flows abundantly.

Once Rachel bears her husband a son, her security is sealed. Of course, Jacob already has ten sons and a daughter when Joseph opens his eyes in the red tent. But knowing that she's the favorite wife, Rachel believes that Joseph will be first in his father's eyes. In fact, she's so secure in Jacob's love that she becomes boldly forthright with him. While Leah artfully frames her suggestion that it's time to embark on the journey, Rachel blurts her opinions right out. Her brazenness jars us, and never more so than when she steals her father's teraphim (the household idols) and tells him that they're polluted by her menstrual blood—a terrible taboo. We're left with the sense that Rachel is a talented midwife and stellar beauty, but beneath those gifts lurks a selfish, devious woman.

WERENRO: THE WILD WOMAN, ONCE DEAD

We first meet Werenro, the exotic redhead, when she announces herself as the one who serves the Grandmother and tosses out morsels of tantalizing lore to the women of Dinah's family as they approach Rebecca's tent. Dinah is smitten with this wild, carefree woman. The next we see of Werenro is a sack of bones, her remains after a brutal murder. After that, she's barely mentioned again for some hundred pages—until a mysterious, heavily veiled dancer appears in the Egyptian palace where Dinah makes her uneasy home. Recognizing Dinah, the stranger reveals herself to be none other than Werenro, having survived the brutality that blinded her and left her face horribly scarred. When Dinah protests that Werenro must be dead and buried, Werenro agrees that she is dead. The dancer Dinah sees is but a shell of the spirit Werenro lost in that attack so many years earlier.

This minor character is so crucial to *The Red Tent* because she spins Dinah around, pointing her toward *life* when Dinah believes herself dead, though still breathing. Declaring there to be no flame left in her own soul, Werenro denies Dinah the same luxury of an easy way out of her sorrow. Dinah's grief has kept her alive, Werenro tells her, and the fire of love still burns within her. Were it not for this chance encounter, Dinah would never open herself to love, would never marry Benia, and would never know peace in her final days.

On Dangerous Ground

The Red Tent has attracted a hefty share of controversy, as some readers embrace its boldness while others decry it as sacrilege.

○ ○ ○

The Red Tent portrays the saga of Jacob's family in a very different way from the Hebrew scriptures. Are the differences problematic? Is Diamant justified in altering the story so drastically?

"DIAMANT MAKES WOMEN THE PRIME MOVERS BEHIND VIRTUALLY EVERY EVENT IN THE STORY— AND REVERSES 3,000 YEARS OF MALE SLANT ON THE BIBLE IN THE PROCESS."

The Red Tent is a fictional novel, not Bible commentary. As a novelist, Diamant has license to cast the biblical story in a different light. The most significant change she makes is recasting the women of the story— especially Leah and Dinah—as the prime movers behind all that happens in the story. In the Bible, the men are the force behind virtually everything that happens. They're the decision-makers, the leaders, the controllers. But in *The Red Tent*, the men are stripped of this power. As a result, the women get credit for a lot of things that we traditionally associate with men in the Bible.

Examples of this switch are everywhere. In the Bible, we read that Laban tricks Jacob by switching Jacob's bride before his wedding—but in *The Red Tent*, the women make the switch themselves. Leah's hand-maiden, Zilpah, scares Rachel so badly about what to expect on her wedding night that Rachel begs Leah to take her place.

In the same way, the women in *The Red Tent* have more control over childbirth than they do in the Bible. One of the running themes of the book of Genesis is the infertility of women—only God opens and closes their wombs. In the Bible, we read that Leah stops giving birth because God closes her womb. But in *The Red Tent*, the women are masters of their own bodies, with the help of their fertility goddesses and their herbal remedies. In Diamant's novel, Leah stops giving birth because she chooses to abstain for a while, until she regains the energy to have more children.

Diamant also gives the women credit for many of the bright ideas the Bible credits to Jacob and Joseph. It's Leah, not Jacob, who understands the mating behavior of the sheep well enough to increase Jacob's flock at the expense of Laban's. In the Bible, Jacob's decision to leave Laban is a significant moment fraught with meaning in the light of the covenant with God, but in *The Red Tent*, the prime motivating factor (aside from Laban's maltreatment) is the plot the women concoct about Laban's abused wife, which humiliates and angers Laban. In *The Red Tent*, Dinah shares Joseph's place among the brothers and teaches him many of the qualities for which he's renowned in the Bible—his storytelling ability, his leadership, his favored status.

In short, Diamant twists virtually everything in the Bible around so that the women have power and the men have none. You can't fault her for it—after all, the Bible is a completely male document: it's a collection of writings by men, largely about men, edited by male editors over the centuries. How can it *not* have been tainted by at least some male bias along the way? *The Red Tent* is a reaction to that, a full working out of biblical women's lives by the women themselves. Diamant is trying to make up for the bias and slant of 3,000 years of male storytelling.

"DIAMANT GOES OVERBOARD IN SHIFTING POWER SO COMPLETELY TO THE WOMEN. HER MOTIVE IS UNDERSTANDABLE, BUT IT DENIES HER A LOT OF CREDIBILITY."

The male narrative of the Bible probably has its biases and leaves out a lot of the women's stories. But that doesn't mean we need to fly all the way to the opposite end of the spectrum and make the women universally all-powerful while leaving every last man in the dust. There's no balance or credibility in that.

Diamant makes major, sweeping changes in virtually every aspect of the story of Jacob's family and the story of Dinah. She leaves no stone unturned. She doesn't let a single man from the story retain any sort of power or control. Not one man in *The Red Tent* has the ability to decide upon any actions himself. In the end, we're left with the sense that Diamant made a lot of these changes simply for the sake of making changes, because she was so intent on correcting the male bias of the Bible and much of the biblical scholarship that's come afterward. Taking such an extreme position costs Diamant—and *The Red Tent*—credibility because she's so intent on overworking every letter of the original biblical text. Some of her points may be valid, and her version of some of the events of the story could be considered valid. But in the end, that all gets lost in the shuffle when we're shaking our heads in disbelief of the overwhelming number of changes Diamant imposes.

"WE CAN SEE *THE RED TENT* AS A MODERN *MIDRASH*—A STORY THAT TRIES TO FILL IN THE GAPS IN THE BIBLE AND MAKE THE STORY OF DINAH MORE RELEVANT TO US TODAY."

Many people believe that *The Red Tent* falls into that body of Hebrew literature known as *midrash*, although Diamant denies that viewpoint. What's *midrash*? Think about how much is left unsaid in the Bible. Classical *midrashim* (the plural, in Hebrew) were stories the ancient rabbis made up to fill in the blanks left by the terse biblical text. The purpose was to make those economical verses more understandable and relevant in a different historical or social context.

Exercising a birthright

Diamant spoke before a large gathering at Temple Beth El in San Mateo, California, in March 2001, referencing a question put to her shortly after *The Red Tent* was released. A Catholic chaplain at Mount Holyoke College asked her, "How did you have the audacity to do this to the Bible?" She responded, "It is my birthright. My audacity is the Jewish approach to Scripture. I approach the Bible as the heir to this tradition of Midrash."

Modern writers continue to weave midrashic tales. So isn't *The Red Tent* one of them? Yes and no. Yes, in that it's based on Genesis, chapters 29–37, wrapped around the Jacob and Joseph sagas, and chock full of historical detail and biblical lore and atmosphere. Is all that enough to make this story a *midrash*? Not necessarily, because *The Red Tent* does stray pretty far from the original biblical text. It makes some startling—to some, unforgivable—leaps, foremost the idea that Dinah's *rape* was really a passionate, starry-eyed love affair. And the entire third section of the novel, "Egypt," is completely from Diamant's imagination—it has no reference point in the Bible at all.

But regardless of whether or not Diamant goes too far, the tradition of *midrash* does give her an extra measure of authorial license. With the large body of tales that are based upon the Bible—but not necessarily factually rooted in the Bible—coming before *The Red Tent*, we can make a little bit more of a case for Diamant's eagerness to reinterpret biblical stories.

"DIAMANT ISN'T ASKING US TO ACCEPT HER VERSION OF THE STORY AS CONCRETE TRUTH. SHE VEERS TO ONE SIDE TO INVITE US TO LOOK FOR THE TRUTH SOMEWHERE IN THE MIDDLE."

Diamant doesn't expect us to believe every word of *The Red Tent* as the "true" story of Dinah. In offering an alternative interpretation, she's asking us to realize that different interpretations are possible.

One issue in *The Red Tent* where this is particularly true is the relationship between Dinah and Shalem. It's tough to avoid the question in discussing Diamant's novel: Was it violent rape and humiliation, as the

Bible says? Or was it a sexual union by eager and mutual consent? Diamant makes the encounter sound like the latter—a passionate love affair, the opposite of a violent rape. In moving to such an extreme, she invites us to ask these questions and look somewhere in the middle. Maybe the encounter between Dinah and Shalem was closer to what we might call date rape today. Maybe it was an act of seduction on Dinah's part.

In short, we'll never know the whole truth about Dinah, whether we look in *The Red Tent* or in Hebrew scripture itself. Regardless of whether or not we agree with Diamant, her novel is an invaluable contribution because it forces us to recognize the haze of mystery that surrounds Dinah's story. Diamant reminds us that her version of the story is just that—one version—and that the truth, if it lies anywhere, probably lies somewhere between *The Red Tent* and the Bible.

○   ○   ○

The Red Tent departs from the Bible by depicting the women of Jacob's family as pagans. Why does Diamant do this? What are the results of the change?

"DIAMANT GOES TOO FAR, FUNDAMENTALLY ALTERING SOME OF THE CENTRAL TENETS OF THE JUDEO-CHRISTIAN TRADITION."

It's not just perplexing, it's downright shocking to read in *The Red Tent* that the women of Jacob's family are still worshipping idols and goddesses, engaging in pagan rituals to celebrate first menses or to usher new life into the tribe. Today, the Judeo-Christian world recognizes Leah, Rachel, and Rebecca not as pagans but as matriarchs of the monotheistic religion that evolved into Judaism, which spawned Christianity and Islam. It's unthinkable that Jacob, who wrestled with an angel of God, who received the legacy of the One God from his father and grandfather, would permit such idolatry within his camp—except perhaps by slaves, handmaidens, and those not yet initiated into the ways of his unseen

God. If Jacob and his sons are so intent on following God's commandment, making sure the men of Shechem are circumcised before they marry women in Jacob's tribe, Jacob surely wouldn't put up with the polytheistic, pantheistic beliefs and rituals of his wives and daughter. Diamant must be wrong, or dreaming. In Diamant's interpretation, the women are hedging their bets by accepting both God and gods, which is contrary to the historical record.

"DIAMANT DOES MAKE SOME BIG CHANGES, BUT AT LEAST SHE'S TRIED TO BACK THEM UP WITH A LOT OF RESEARCH."

When Diamant was writing *The Red Tent*, she did extensive research on the semi-nomadic people of the ancient biblical world. At the very least, we can consider her investigations a good-faith effort—and we might go so far as to trust her interpretation. As the women's rituals concern bodily matters, their modesty would force them to perform their rites in private—that is, away from male eyes. Diamant tells us that the men in the story know nothing of their ceremonies in the red tent. She tells us that Jacob's wives do what they're called upon to do for him and his God, and that Jacob ignores their goddess worship. It sounds like a practical arrangement forged under difficult circumstances. We have to give these wily women some credit. Leah and even Rachel humor and flatter their husband and give lip service to his God's power, but their emotional and spiritual lives are strictly among women and children. This issue raises questions about how Jacob's sons are educated in his religious beliefs. But what's really at issue here isn't male spirituality—it's about what the *women* practice in the red tent and believe in their hearts.

"THE WOMEN HAVE NO CHOICE—JACOB DOESN'T LET THEM IN ON HIS FATHERS' RELIGION. THE WOMEN'S IDOLS REFLECT THEIR OWN CONCERNS."

As we know from the Bible, Jacob inherits his monotheistic religion from his father. But the women are never privy to this new faith. Dinah doesn't receive religious instruction, whereas her brothers do— they know who their father's God is, they circumcise their sons, and so on. But the women still have their own concerns, especially those related to childbirth, fertility, and their role in the household. They have to compensate somehow, so they practice their own belief system.

The women's main preoccupations concern matters of their own bodies, as distinct from men. Not surprisingly, their sense of spirituality is tied intimately to the image of Earth as a nurturing mother just like them. They fear (and must have ceremonies to dispel) demons, such as the ones who hunger for newborn lives. These desert women also put their faith in a range of fertility goddesses in the hopes of helping themselves conceive when they're barren or preventing conception when their bodies are worn down from childbearing. For example, Dinah talks about how Sarai, Jacob's grandmother, was so favored by the goddess Innana that Innana gave her the ability to birth a son far beyond her childbearing years. That's a powerful god to be reckoned with.

So Diamant makes it clear that Jacob's women worship Innana, goddess mother, and a whole other host of other gods and goddesses who specifically affect the matters that concern them most—pregnancy, childbirth, crop, and livestock to feed and clothe the family. It's unlikely that these women, bound so closely to things of the earth, would understand God in the same way as Jacob and his fathers, who have entirely different concerns. An entity so abstract and formless must seem like a frivolous luxury to these women, in light of the issues they deal with day by day and birth by birth. The *teraphim*, the household idols Rachel steals for the journey, feel much more direct and practical to them.

"DIAMANT USES THE WOMEN'S RELIGION AS A WAY TO SHOW THE WOMEN'S WORLD AS COMPLETE AND SEPARATE FROM THE MEN'S WORLD."

It's clear from the start that Diamant's intent in writing the novel was to portray biblical women's lives as completely as the Bible portrays men's lives. To that end, she uses the women's religion as a central pillar that unifies and supports the women's lives as completely separate from the men.

The women in *The Red Tent* live by a completely different calendar than the men. Diamant's novel is about women's time, whereas the Bible is about men's time. The women in the novel measure their time by weeks—at the end of each week they make sacrifices to the queen of heaven, which prefigures something Jewish women still do today when they bake bread—and by months, on new moons, when they all bleed at the same time and enjoy sweets and storytelling in the red tent.

Just as the Bible provides us little inside information about women, the men in *The Red Tent* are clueless about what their women really think and do in private. The women's paganism and idol worship is the primary symbol of how the women's world is completely separate from the men's. When Dinah gets her first period, the women celebrate a pagan ceremony—yet the men, aside from a few rumblings in the camp, seem completely unaware of what the women are up to.

We may wonder whether Diamant sidesteps the issue of whether or not the men are aware of the women's religion. She doesn't address it in any great detail. But it's unclear whether we should see that as a flaw in her novel or whether Diamant avoids it purposefully—perhaps her point is that the men really don't know or care much about what the women do under the cover of the red tent. The saddest outcome of the men's ignorance of the women's private lives is that we know the women's religion will die with Dinah.

○　○　○

Dinah's primary concern is that she has been forgotten through the millennia. Is she really forgotten? Or does Diamant rescue her from obscurity?

"DINAH IS MEMORABLE FROM THE START, BUT ESPECIALLY AFTER READING *THE RED TENT*."

Diamant has given us a rare glimpse into the daily life of a girl who's the fulfillment of the dreams of other women in the Bible. Dinah, daughter of Jacob, is special from the moment of her conception. In the novel, Leah is exhausted from bearing so many children, and when she finds herself pregnant yet again, she quietly looks for fennel seeds in the hope that they'll induce a miscarriage. But Rachel, a knowing midwife, discerns that the child in Leah's womb is a girl, the one for whom they've all been waiting. Dinah is born into wild rejoicing and is cherished by each of her father's four wives, even if her father himself barely notices her existence. All through her years before her first marriage, Dinah lives in the loving environment of four women, eleven brothers, and a slew of other clan members. Although Dinah isn't recognized by her family thirty years later, the young women of the clan continue to relate the story of her life, even to this "stranger" in their midst. A niece later gives birth to a girl, naming her for this Dinah of memory in the clan. She's not forgotten among the women in the Bible. What about by readers?

No reader of *The Red Tent* can forget the earth-bound, primitive rituals the mothers perform when Dinah comes of age, or the mothers' feral rejoicing that she's become a woman capable of bearing children herself. No reader will forget Dinah's asking for a mirror and knife as she stands upon the bricks to deliver her own baby. No reader can forget the image of Dinah in the arms of her beloved Shalem, covered in his blood. Because of Diamant's novel, women's book groups have been gathering in homes and churches and synagogues to remember Dinah, and they appear en masse whenever Diamant has a book signing. *The Red Tent* has lifted Dinah out of anonymity and given her a central place in the emotional roll call of biblical women.

"DINAH JUST ISN'T THAT COMPELLING—SHE REMAINS A PASSIVE VICTIM, EVEN AFTER WE READ A FULL-LENGTH NOVEL THAT TELLS HER SIDE OF THE STORY."

In the prologue to *The Red Tent*, Dinah says that she's merely a "footnote" between the stories of two great men—Jacob, her father, and Joseph, her brother. And if people remember her at all, it's as a victim. But it's hard to imagine any other way to remember Dinah—she *is* a victim, whether we interpret the central drama in her life as a rape or a torrid love affair. Taking Diamant's premise—that Dinah and Shalem shared a rare and beautiful romance, mutual from the first glance—Dinah still comes out the victim of her brothers' greed and violent extremes and of her father's neglect.

Dinah is buffeted by circumstance, such as when her mother-in-law's cold refusal to allow the name of Shalem, whom they both love, to be spoken in the great house. Dinah mourns alone, has no one to turn to for relief from her blood-soaked nightmares. Her son coldly rejects her, becomes a stranger to her when he's sent away to school, and relates to her as if she were an underling and he were a grown man, full of himself. When Dinah returns to Canaan to bid farewell to her dying father, she's denied the satisfaction of hearing her name spoken, even when Jacob curses his sons for their egregious behavior at Shechem. She goes unrecognized among her own kin. Joseph confirms that the house of Jacob has forgotten Dinah's name. Even among her own people, it's as though Dinah never lived.

If Diamant's intention was to show women as agents of their own destiny, it certainly didn't turn out that way in Dinah's life. *The Red Tent* isn't enough to salvage Dinah's image, and she will always remain a sad, shadowy figure whose name is never uttered among the great women of Hebrew scripture—Sarah, Rebecca, Leah, Rachel, and Miriam—or even among the lesser names like Deborah, Hannah, Ruth, Naomi, and Esther. All those women performed heroic deeds, whereas Dinah is remembered—if at all—for loving unwisely and arousing murderous wrath in her brothers. Even though *The Red Tent* is a phenomenon now, in the larger picture of literary history it'll never come close to the Bible in terms of readership or credibility—so Dinah will remain forgotten.

"EVEN IF DINAH IS LARGELY FORGOTTEN, AT LEAST HER REPUTATION IS CLEANER THAN MANY OF THE OTHER WOMEN IN JACOB'S FAMILY."

Look at the matriarchs depicted in this novel—women who will be remembered as long as Western culture exists. Each of them has a sullied reputation. Rebecca plays favorites between her two sons, deceives her husband, and is grossly unkind to her daughters-in-law and granddaughters. Leah deceives Jacob, selfishly posing as his bride after he labors like a slave for so long to win Rachel. Her deception condemns him to another lengthy period of servitude. Rachel, on top of all her jealousy and unkindness toward Leah, is a common thief. She takes property from her father's house, cruelly denying him the safety he seeks from the household gods. Yet Rachel and these other women are remembered— their names are uttered in Jewish prayers to this day.

If all those women are unforgettable, despite their flaws and misde-meanors, all the more should Dinah be remembered. Whether in the Bible or Diamant's novel, Dinah does *nothing* evil or duplicitous. She brings unbridled joy to her mothers and to Shalem, aids women in tra-vail, saves the lives of babies in houses both great and common, dutifully mothers her son as long as she is allowed to, and never does anything to hurt anyone deliberately. This selflessness is heroic in its own light — and thus, Dinah remains memorable.

The rabbis of old, in the first through seventh centuries B.C., worried about Dinah, about whether she'd be remembered in the line of Jacob. There's a *midrash* about Dinah that tells us she *didn't* fade into obscurity, that in fact she had a daughter, a girl named As-naat. If that name sounds familiar, think about Joseph's wife, whose son Dinah is called to deliver. According to the *midrash*, Joseph marries his niece, the daughter of Dinah (a common occurrence at the time). Joseph and As-naat are the parents of two sons, Efraem and Menashe. Traditional Jewish fathers of today are familiar with this *midrash* as they bless their children each Sab-bath eve. With their hands held lovingly over the heads of their children, the fathers ask God to make their daughters like Sarah, Rebecca, Rachel, and Leah. And they ask God to make their sons like Efraem and Men-ashe. Although her name may not be mentioned, just as Jacob failed to mention her name as he closed his eyes for the last time, Dinah is remembered in the names of her alleged grandsons every single Sabbath.

"THE END OF *THE RED TENT* CUTS DINAH OFF FROM WOMEN'S TIME, FROM THE STORYTELLING TRADITION OF THE FIRST HALF OF THE NOVEL."

The first two sections of *The Red Tent* give us a long look into women's time, measured in weeks and months by the cycles of the moon, and fea-tures the women's storytelling. But even though the women have the stronger mechanism for continuity, Rachel and Leah have only one daughter between them — Dinah, on whom everything rests.

Even though the men in the Bible assume the ultimate storytelling responsibilities, the women in *The Red Tent* take that duty upon them-selves. Granted, Diamant doesn't show us much about what goes on in the men's side of the camp. But regardless of what remains undisclosed about the lives of men, the women are concerned with preserving the past and predicting the future. When Dinah goes to Egypt, in some ways it's the end of time for her. She can't allow herself to think or talk about the past. And she doesn't bother to consider the future because she's so sure she has none. This exile in Egypt cuts her off from women's time.

Dinah's exile also means she's severed from her roots, and thus the women's story and their religion end with her. The female descendants of Dinah's family remember her, but they scarcely believe the story themselves: "the story of Dinah was too terrible to be forgotten. As long as the memory of Jacob lived, my name would be remembered." In the end, it's the mechanism of masculine storytelling that preserves Dinah's story—albeit a distorted version.

○   ○   ○

Is Shalem and Dinah's love affair in *The Red Tent* believable in light of the biblical account about rape? Does it turn the novel into a pulp romance? What about Dinah's marriage to Benia?

"YES, DINAH'S WORLD IS A HIGHLY SEXUAL ONE, BUT IT'S MORE LIKELY THAT THE BIBLE DOWNPLAYED THE SEX THAN THAT DIAMANT OVERDID IT."

The biblical account doesn't really matter in the world of *The Red Tent*. Diamant is a novelist and has no obligation to tell the story in the same way Genesis does. Dinah is a healthy adolescent girl who has lived her life in two spheres, both of which propelled her into precocious sexuality. The first, her social circle, is a whole battalion of brothers older than she. She watches as they ripen into manhood and explore their sexuality. From an early age, she observes that her oldest brother Reuben is attracted to the handmaiden, Bilhah, who at the same time is one of the four mothers. The other, more direct sphere of influence is the frank sexuality of the mothers themselves. Everyone in the camp knows which of the four women Jacob chooses on any given night, and he seems to be a man of considerable zest. Equally robust are Rachel and Leah and Bilhah, though Zilpah is more reserved.

In short, female rhythms and appetites are apparent among the women throughout Dinah's childhood and adolescence. All the women celebrate puberty rites as a community. There's even a certain sash, like the one Dinah's cousin Tabea wears, that indicates to the world that a girl has come of age. It's all out in the open. Dinah's informal apprenticeship to Rachel invites her to witness and even assist in childbirth before she's of age to conceive a child herself. As we see in Rachel, as soon as a girl has her first menses, she's fodder for a marriage straight away. In this carnal environment, it's not surprising that Dinah would fall into bed with a young man she sees and loves instantly. In the end, Diamant's retelling probably doesn't sexualize the story any more than any other modern account of Dinah would.

"DIAMANT PUTS A MODERN SPIN ON DINAH'S STORY, AND SHE DEFINITELY SEXES IT UP."

In *The Red Tent*, Diamant puts a twenty-first century spin on a 3,500-year-old tale. It's unlikely that a girl like Dinah, protected by so many mothers and brothers, would be allowed to wander through the marketplace of the big city and strike up a tacit agreement with a strange boy— then, on their second meeting, play house and indulge in mad, passionate lovemaking for four days, without a worry about her future. Shalem is a stranger from a different culture and a member of a higher social class, whereas Dinah comes from a close-knit, semi-nomadic clan. It's unthinkable that she'd turn her back on her family and so easily fall into such a torrid love affair, which she equates with the carefully arranged, clan-based marriages in her own culture. In the end, the story comes across like a modern soap opera or B-list romance novel—it's unrealistic and sensationalized. Diamant trivializes a truly tragic and heartrending story in order to titillate, in order to sell books.

"DINAH AND SHALEM'S RELATIONSHIP IS ROMANTIC, NOT TORRID. BESIDES, DINAH FINDS FULLER LOVE LATER IN LIFE, WITH BENIA."

Dinah and Shalem's romance isn't unrealistic—it's splendidly romantic. The love they share is sweet, filled with tenderness and humor, love, and respect, and deeply passionate. Shalem doesn't rape her—he adores her, and it's entirely mutual. It's young love in its purest sense. And the idea that the two "lived in sin" isn't that relevant, because marriage ceremonies were virtually nonexistent at that time. A couple might be brought together by their fathers, or they'd find one another on their own, go off together, and immediately live as a married couple. That's exactly what occurs in Dinah's life. It just so happens that she finds a wonderful prince charming who treasures her as she treasures him. As much as we might not want to admit it, the magnetic pull of such intense love and sexual attraction outweighs family loyalty. Doesn't everybody want what Dinah and Shalem find together, at least when we're young?

But it's different later in life. After years alone, Dinah never expects to love again, until Benia comes into her life. Though they're past their prime, their attraction is physical. Dinah describes finding "wells of desire and passion" that she never dreamed she had within her. What these two share is a total relationship, more in line with our modern concept of a healthy marriage. They establish a full life together, and Dinah is delighted to nest in the first house she can claim as her own. She and Benia enjoy quiet moments, stargazing along the river, sharing their most intimate life histories and thoughts, their victories and defeats in their own work. It's a marriage of mind and body, heart and soul. Even if Shalem had lived, his and Dinah's superheated passion would have cooled, and a man of his position would have taken other wives and concubines. That relationship, sadly, would be doomed in any imagined outcome.

The Red Tent is a novel by and about women.
Is it fair in its treatment of men? How might
a male reader respond to the book?

"THE NOVEL IS STAUNCHLY ANTI-MALE AND WOULD UNDERSTANDABLY TURN OFF A MALE READER."

Open-minded men might be able to use *The Red Tent* to try to ease their way into the female psyche and to try to understand how women feel about their bodies, their reproductive cycles, and their gender roles. But Diamant delves into these topics so far that the novel probably turns off the vast majority of male readers. Admittedly, the women in the novel are endlessly fascinated with menstruation and childbirth. The first section of the novel deals with little else except landing a husband (or sharing a sister's husband), cavorting on blankets in smelly tents, getting pregnant or avoiding pregnancy, having baby boys, or helping other women have baby boys, all of whom must be circumcised. Probably none of this material would be appealing to most men.

What's more, male readers would probably also take offense at the extent to which the women of the novel—and Diamant herself—emasculate men, wielding their power through deception. Take Rebecca, for instance. In her witchy manner, she turns poor Isaac into a dotty old fool—Isaac, whose name means laughter. She banishes him from her tent and relegates him to a distant home, tended by a nameless, veiled servant. Jacob doesn't fare much better. The women conspire to switch brides on him after he has labored for so long, and we're supposed to believe he wouldn't even notice until he got Leah on the blanket? And Laban is portrayed as a thoroughly despicable character—greedy, manipulative, and easily duped, with no redeeming qualities. Joseph is unscrupulous, power-hungry, unforgiving, and illiterate. Simon and Levi are bloodthirsty hoodlums. Shalem, the starry-eyed prince, has a dubious reputation—lover or rapist? Re-mose comes across as an arrogant, self-centered little tyrant. In the end, Diamant's ceaseless focus on empowering women at the expense of every single man in the novel would probably turn off most male readers.

"EVEN THOUGH WOMEN ARE THE FOCUS, *THE RED TENT* ISN'T A MAN-HATING BOOK."

Benia, for one, is a strong male role model in the novel. He represents our archetype of the *good* man—handsome, self-effacing, endlessly patient, and all-forgiving. He has talent in his massive hands, producing works of surpassing beauty, and he overflows with joy at beautiful things in the marketplace. He's a generous lover, not just a hotheaded, hormone-driven male, which is what we suspect of Shalem. Benia has uncommon insight, as we see in his interpretation of the ring Dinah receives from her mother, via her brother Judah. When Dinah is puzzled as to how the ring (once Rachel's) came to be her mother's and finally hers, it's Benia who interprets the symbolism. He holds Dinah's hand to the light, examines the beautiful ring, and suggests that it's meant as a token of forgiveness—a sign that Rachel has overcome her hatred for her sister, Leah. Benia, having been through tragedy himself and forgiven those who wronged him, understands the significance of the ring. He sobs at Dinah's death. He's the perfect model of the strong, artistic, sensitive man.

But Benia's not the only decent man in *The Red Tent*. Joseph, who encounters great cruelty from his brothers, possesses redeeming qualities as well. Both early in his life, when he's a friend to Dinah, and later, when they return to their father's deathbed and part at Memphis, Joseph displays great tenderness, saying he will always think of Dinah. Diamant also portrays Judah and Reuben as good men, not caught up in the blood revenge their other two brothers stir up. Even Esau—who's entitled to his wrath toward Jacob for stealing his birthright, who by ancient Near Eastern tradition has every right to wage war against his duplicitous brother—throws his arms around his brother and eases the enmity between them. And Nehesi, the wise and faithful servant of Dinah's mother-in-law, remains a staunch, faithful, and wise advisor throughout his life. Dinah, her mother-in-law, and Re-mose could barely have existed without his loyalty.

Together these men more than make up for some of Diamant's less flattering portrayals of other male characters. In the end, her portrait of biblical characters focuses on women but remains balanced in its treatment of men.

"DIAMANT ACTUALLY MAKES QUITE AN EFFORT TO STEP OUTSIDE THE LIMITATIONS OF HER FIRST-PERSON NARRATOR AND GET INSIDE THE MINDS OF SOME OF THE MEN."

Because *The Red Tent* is overwhelmingly a women's story, Diamant isn't obligated to get inside the males' minds or even to portray them objectively. That's why some of the biblical patriarchs we traditionally admire look rather anemic in *The Red Tent*. Diamant has said that it was her intention to depict biblical women not as victims but as agents of their own destiny. In light of that, she *must* allow them to demonstrate control over their environment and over the men who are indisputably in power. We've looked at the clever, subtle ways both Leah and Rachel make their wishes known to Jacob, leading him to believe that his decisions are his own. But now we have to examine whether Diamant's fair to the men in the book. Again, we view them through a prism that may distort reality— through Dinah's eyes and ears. One of the complications of writing in the first person is that it's impossible for Diamant to give us a direct window into any scenes that the first-person narrator doesn't witness.

But Diamant does exactly this—using some narrative tricks she hopes we won't notice. There are a few scenes that Dinah couldn't possibly have witnessed or even learned of by hearsay. They're private conversations among men or musings within the head of a man. The first comes shortly after Jacob meets Rachel and Leah. The narration describes what Jacob observes about each of the women and how he courts each according to her own needs and personality. Shortly after that, Jacob and Laban discuss the bride price for Rachel. It's unlikely that such a delicate, male-centered negotiation would've taken place in front of the women. Diamant is only able to convey this scene to us by allowing Zilpah to spy on the conversation and report it in gleeful detail. It's harder to explain the scene in which Eliphaz comes as a messenger from his father, Esau. The novel describes how Jacob "railed and wept" in his heart, how he felt trapped and cursed himself for his preoccupation with the demons and angels who haunted him at the Jabbok River. Toward the end of the novel there's the dramatic confrontation between Joseph and Re-mose in which they each acknowledge their relationship with Dinah. In just a few pages of dialogue, we get inside the minds of both men in this scene.

Daughter of History

Diamant has funneled a lifetime's curiosity about her religion into six books about Jewish life and now a bestselling novel.

○ ○ ○

A RECENT INTERVIEWER VISITED Anita Diamant in her simple white frame home near Boston. The two sipped tea and chatted across a Formica table, perched on kitchen chairs straight out of the 1950s. Not the glamorous digs you'd expect for a bestselling writer.

As readers, we tend to have a fascination with the personal lives of authors whose books we admire. We want to know . . . is she married? Children? Has she overcome dizzying obstacles? Suffered from writer's block? Was she born in a mansion—or better yet, in a manger? What are the spicy tidbits in her life that we can nibble on? Applying these tantalizing questions as a measure of Anita Diamant, we find yards and yards of durable fabric stitched together in a mostly satisfying domestic and professional life. She's married, has a teenage daughter, is active in her synagogue, and works hard at her writing. That's the life she wears comfortably, but we want to see the underpinnings. We're eager to view, up close and personal, what in her apparently unremarkable life has shaped her six nonfiction books and two novels—especially what gave birth to *The Red Tent*.

One fact must be mentioned immediately. Diamant is the daughter of Holocaust survivors. While she rarely speaks of this aspect of her background, we can only guess that it's had a great effect on how she views religion, politics, relationships, and love—and on how she chooses her subjects. She spent her early years in New Jersey, then moved with her parents to the fresh air of Colorado. Although her family was ethnically and culturally Jewish, they weren't religious, and she had a meager Jewish education—surprising when we consider that all of her books, fiction and nonfiction, deal with religious themes. It wasn't until her high-school years in Colorado that Diamant's family even joined a synagogue, and still later, when she was engaged to a man preparing to convert to Judaism, that she began to study.

That study evolved into a lifetime of Jewish learning. The resources for such elementary explorations were few. In fact, when Diamant asked her rabbi to recommend a book on basic, practical Judaism for non-Orthodox Jews, he advised her to write the book herself. She did, and that book was *The New Jewish Wedding*, published in 1985 and since revised. As Diamant says, "I wrote my way into understanding what I needed to learn."

Diamant had been writing since childhood, but writing wasn't the career she expected to grow into. Acting is what she wanted, but as is often the case, that career didn't work out. After completing degrees in comparative and English literature at Washington University in St. Louis and SUNY-Binghamton in New York, Diamant thought she'd be an English professor for a living and a poet for love. But as Dinah experiences, that's not what the "gods" had in store for her. By her mid-twenties, Diamant was editing for Boston-area newspapers and magazines. Later, she wrote for numerous national magazines on everything from celebrity profiles to family life essays to sports commentaries. Her first published poem was about basketball. Not yet a fiction writer at that point, Diamant says of that period in her life, "Journalism satisfied both my love of writing and my need to get paid."

Eclectic tastes

Diamant offers quite a varied list of authors to whom she returns time and again for inspiration. It's a curious pack, including the Latin American novelists and poets Gabriel García Márquez and Pablo Neruda, the eighteenth-century English novelist Jane Austen, the groundbreaking nineteenth-century poet Walt Whitman, the food writer M.F.K. Fisher, and the rabbi and theologian Abraham Joshua Heschel.

The voyage of a writer is difficult to track, as the path through the waters may zigzag and leave a turbulent wake. We can only pick up the trail here and there, such as in Diamant's essay about her husband's conversion to the Jewish faith, which engendered her own extensive studies. The essay, titled "My Conversion Story," describes the strange feeling of waiting in a parked car on a residential street outside a urologist's office while her husband was inside undergoing a symbolic circumcision. (It's not as horrifying as it might sound, since it only involves taking a drop of blood of a man who's already circumcised.) But it makes us wonder if this landmark experience might have led Diamant, some twenty years later, to Dinah's story. What we *do* know is that over these twenty years Diamant has written six handbooks on contemporary Jewish practice. The last, on end-of-life issues and death customs, was written while she was still in mourning over her father's death.

Shortly afterward, at age forty, Diamant relished a change of course, turning to fiction. Out of that sea change came *The Red Tent*, then *Good Harbor*, and then the workings of her third novel, not yet published. Diamant finds fiction wholly satisfying, and she has no plans to return to nonfiction in the near future — unless she chooses to write a book about *Chayim Mayim* (life waters), the *mikvah* or Jewish ritual bath that she and her husband have dreamed into reality in Boston.

Dreaming is indispensable to a writer. Diamant daydreams and writes at home, which may be either in Boston or in a seaside vacation cabin in Gloucester, Massachusetts, the place where she put the finishing touches on *The Red Tent*. That novel required enormous amounts of research at Radcliffe College, which awarded Diamant a fellowship, a small office, and access to the entire Harvard University library system. On top of this research, Diamant spent scores of hours in the library as a visiting scholar at Brandeis University. In a sense, the librarians at these institutions were midwives to Diamant herself during the three years she labored to deliver the novel to her publisher.

The novel's delivery was easy compared to the birth of Diamant's daughter in 1986. In her essay on Emilia's birth, which culminated in an unexpected Caesarian section, Diamant described the overwhelming euphoria she and her husband shared as they gazed at the peacefully sleeping baby. She said, "We loved each other like survivors of a shipwreck." The currents haven't always been gentle since then. Fifteen months later, their marriage was on rocky shores. In a candid essay, Diamant wrote of the arduous work with a marriage counselor that steadied her and her husband for smooth sailing once again.

She's also written about her own religious and spiritual journey and her gratitude for the simple things she loves—ocean sunsets, fresh-picked vegetables, dancing dolphins, pie baking, and the voice of the singer James Taylor, which reminds her of beaches and bicycles. She's gratified by the steady success of her Jewish handbooks and stunned by how generously people have embraced *The Red Tent*.

Was it daunting to write her second novel, when avid readers wanted her to continue her "franchise" in biblical tales? Diamant speaks of a publisher who told her *The Good Harbor* shouldn't be her second novel. But her response was, "This *is* my second novel. There's no should or shouldn't; that's what came out next." She goes on to say that failing to follow her instincts would be doing violence to herself. Diamant's instincts seem to be sound, as *The Good Harbor* has been launched and well received, and her ship is steady as she goes.

In God's Country

To recreate the Gaza of biblical times, Diamant goes beyond Genesis and back to the archaeological record.

○   ○   ○

GEOGRAPHICAL

When reading *The Red Tent*, it might be useful to imagine a mental map of the ancient Near East to gain a clearer picture of the distances Dinah and her family travel. Geographers describe the entire area as about the size of New Jersey. In Diamant's novel, Jacob's clan begins in Haran, a city in the Paddan-aram region in northwestern Mesopotamia. It's roughly equivalent to today's Syria and Iraq. The Jabbok River, where Jacob has his physical and mental encounter with the mysterious stranger, is a tributary of the Jordan River that lies halfway between the Dead Sea and the Sea of Galilee. The trek from Haran to Succoth is a distance of roughly 350 miles (an educated guess, as precise mileage is difficult to pinpoint).

Jacob and his clan settle for two years in a place called Succoth, dallying long enough for several of Dinah's brothers to marry local women and many more babies to be born. In the middle of their stay in that village, they dip down further into Canaan. (Think of Canaan as a corridor between today's Asia and Africa.) Their purpose is to visit Mamre, Isaac and Rebecca's home, a distance of some sixty miles from Succoth. After the barley festival, the family returns to Succoth, with Dinah following a few months later. When Jacob's herds grow too large for the land to support them, the clan moves on to the rich green valley, a "suburb" of Shechem, site of Dinah's great ill-fated romance.

41

Shechem is a major Canaanite city with heavy Egyptian influence. The city bustles at the eastern end of the pass between Mount Ebal and Mount Gerizim, an area that today lies within the borders of the state of Israel. It's on the road to Bethlehem that Rachel dies giving birth to Benjamin and must be buried along the side of the road so the family can continue on their journey. Dinah is no longer among them. After the destruction of Shechem, she follows her mother-in-law to Egypt.

To make the journey to Egypt, Dinah travels down the Nile to the cities of Memphis and finally Thebes, where she makes her uneasy home. During Dinah's years there, Thebes thrives along the banks of the Nile as the capital of Egypt and the chief city of Upper Egypt. Glancing at a map, we see that Upper Egypt is south of Lower Egypt, which seems to defy logic until we realize that the Nile River that ribbons the area is highly unusual—it's the only major river that flows south to north rather than the other way around. So the mouth or head of the river, in the south of the country, becomes the "top" of Egypt, peering up at its bottom half. Picture Egypt standing on its head—and achieving all that conquest, wealth, and refined culture anyway.

CULTURAL AND HISTORICAL

The Red Tent takes place during the period of time somewhere between 1800 and 1500 B.C., within what archaeologists call the Middle Bronze Age. From the start, it's important to note that many of the cultural and historical details of the period are hazy and still open to speculation and debate among scholars.

Scholars differ on the dating of the Middle Bronze Age, but Diamant settles on 1500 B.C. Though this is the place, it's not yet the time for the incredible cultural contribution of the Phoenician alphabet, which occurred a few hundred years later. The remarkably avant garde Code of Hammurabi, a system of justice designed to prevent the strong from oppressing the weak, has been in effect for two centuries in neighboring Mesopotamia.

The Hebrews live on the fringes of the great civilizations of their day. Despite evidence to the contrary—Shechem being one blatant example—the Hebrews are by no means a lawless people. We're hundreds of years away from the law given at Sinai, which defines and solidifies the covenant between God and the Israelite people. Nonetheless, Hebrews in Dinah's day follow a civil legal code—although it's not as detailed as the Code of Hammurabi and differs from one area to another. The laws of the city of Ur, for example, would favor Rachel's taking the *teraphim*, whereas the laws in Haran wouldn't. Laws of birthright and inheritance are set but all too often violated amid the convoluted family disputes told in the book of Genesis.

Around 1720 B.C., Egypt falls to the Semitic Hyksos, whom the native Egyptians view as barbarians. Even after the Hyksos are expelled in 1500 B.C., their influence is responsible for the establishment of the New Kingdom that will reign for 500 years. While not popular with Egyptians, Hyksos rule benefits the Hebrews, because the Hebrews and Hyksos share an "otherness" that renders the new king more favorably disposed to a fellow Semite like Joseph rising in the ranks.

The world of the patriarchs is one in which few are literate, not even the leaders. In *The Red Tent*, Diamant depicts Joseph as illiterate—a plot device to enable Re-mose, Dinah's son, to be Joseph's scribe and thereby bring Dinah and Joseph into the same realm. But scholars and Bible traditionalists dispute this illiteracy factor. They're reluctant to see one of the great fathers of the faith—a man who's risen to such heights by his insightful dream interpretation—as intellectually stunted. Few dispute the notion that ordinary people, such as Jacob and the women in his family, would be unable to read or write.

In such an illiterate environment, knowledge of family relationships and traditions, tribal history and laws, are passed from one generation to the next orally. Information often is conveyed in rhyme or song, accompanied by lyre—a small, portable harp-like instrument. The language in which these songs are sung is today a subject of debate. Scholars generally assume that the patriarchs and their families spoke Aramean, but some argue that the Aramean language group wouldn't appear in the area for nearly two centuries after the events of *The Red Tent*. In short, we don't know for sure what language the characters use to convey their heritage and dreams to one another.

Though preliterate and clearly not as advanced as their neighbors (the Egyptians and Mesopotamians), these semi-nomadic people of *The Red Tent* are far from uncultured. They understand animal husbandry, planting and sowing, healing arts, and certainly reproduction. They practice metalworking, pottery making, stone carving, spinning wool and linen, weaving, and a variety of decorative arts. Male and female roles are clearly defined. Women draw water from the well for human and animal consumption—a lucky break for Rachel, who meets her beloved at the well. Women also are responsible for sewing and pitching tents with each encampment, which is an important job among these semi-nomadic peoples.

The tents are made of woven strips of black, brown, and reddish goat hairs and skin, with little furniture inside. Woven mats serve as rugs, seats, tables, and beds. When Diamant mentions the "blankets" as the beds upon which so much activity occurs in *The Red Tent*, she's really referring to these woven mats.

Diamant never gives us a clue that lions commonly prey on sheep during early biblical times. Lions only become extinct in the region toward the end of the Middle Ages. Hence, the biblical symbol of peace: the lion and the lamb lying down together.

An Unlikely Bestseller

The Red Tent's phenomenal success stems not from a marketing campaign but from the word of mouth of its readers.

○ ○ ○

THE RED TENT **WAS A BESTSELLER** of a different breed, a book that took a different path from the potboilers that zoom their way to the top of the *New York Times* list. Diamant researched for years and wrote her novel without an advance, learning and honing the craft of novel writing on the fly after so many years in journalism. Several agents read the manuscript and declined to represent the book to publishers.

When an agent sent *The Red Tent* to St. Martin's Press, it finally landed on the desk of an appreciative editor. Although we tend to think of Diamant's novel as a women's story, the editor who ushered it through publication was a man insightful enough to see the book's charm and potential. Unfortunately, this editor left St. Martin's partway through the production schedule for *The Red Tent*, leaving the book "orphaned" without an editor to nurse it through the fragile post-production process. It was released in 1997 to a resounding silence—no advertising and few reviews. The hardcover sold barely 10,000 copies, largely on the coattails of Diamant's modest but steady reputation for her handbooks to modern Jewish life. Her novel seemed doomed to a bloodless and silent death.

But then the publisher Picador USA came to the rescue, plucking *The Red Tent* from its road to obscurity by reissuing the novel in a striking, oversized trade paperback. At Diamant's urging, St. Martin's snatched the leftover hardcovers out of the remaindered pile and sent free copies to nearly 500 female rabbis, along with a letter of endorsement from a nationally prominent rabbi; then to another 500 rabbis, female *and* male; and finally to hundreds of women ministers, book group leaders, and mega-booksellers that support book groups. At long last, *The Red Tent* began to collect reviews in the religious and mainstream press, which eventually landed it on the independent booksellers' list of most recommended books. All this energy breathed new life into a nearly dead tome.

To top it off, Diamant made a three-year circuit of Jewish community events and book fairs, and her exhaustive and exhausting efforts have certainly paid off. *The Red Tent* has now sold 1.5 million copies and counting, with an apparently eternal future in liberal Jewish and Christian circles. It's not only a literary success but also a promotional darling that's forced the publishing industry to perk up and reckon with the incredible power of the religious media, independent booksellers, and avid women's book clubs.

And *The Red Tent* isn't limited to English readers by any means. It's been translated into nineteen languages, and foreign editions are available countries around the globe. In May 2001, film rights were sold to the independent film companies Palomar Pictures and Oculus Pictures, who want to adapt Diamant's novel as a joint venture. A producer from Palomar and director from Oculus have been assigned, but the film has yet to be cast. In an appearance Diamant made in March 2001 at a synagogue in San Mateo, California, people were intrigued to hear about the possibility of a film. Audience members asked who would play Dinah — Julia Roberts? Diamant laughed at the suggestion but offered no answer. Perhaps she thought that no one in biblical times could have had such perfect teeth.

A process of learning

Diamant on whether fiction is a greater challenge to her than writing nonfiction: "It's more open-ended. I have confidence in my nonfiction — I've written six books. I know what that kind of book is shaped like. With novels, you don't know where they're going to go. All writing is a process of learning. I learned you have to cut and cut and cut. Big sections were in *Good Harbor* that died a healthy death, a good death, but it took me a long time to let go."

Julia Roberts aside, at this time there's no word on a release date for the film. What is known is that the rights sold for a sum in the mid-to-high six figures, and the film is listed in trade publications as a tragedy-romance. No mention of the biblical setting, but if the screenplay follows the novel closely, we're going to see a lot of begetting and dozens of babies born on screen. But we can only speculate on how the film might end up nearly unrecognizable to readers who love the novel and have their own vision of its characters and landscape.

So after all the history of *The Red Tent*, what have people thought of it? A quick glance at the online bookstores shows a staggering 1,000-plus reader reviews for the novel. It's probably fair to say that the ordinary reader wouldn't bother writing a review if he or she didn't either love or hate the novel. And indeed, the majority of reviewers have praised it highly. They point out that Diamant has made the biblical cast of characters come alive as they never have before, and that she's brought earthy female rituals out of the shadows of secrecy and shame. They applaud the novel for demonstrating what the Bible might have been like if written by women, for showing what it must have been like for women trying to bridge paganism and monotheism. Such words as "magnificent," "breathtaking," "awesome," "empowering," "intriguing," and "inventive" are sprinkled through hundreds of reviews.

The Red Tent has not won universal acceptance. Some who see the Bible as the unerring word of God have taken offense at Diamant's creative interpretations. One reviewer described the novel as a vehicle for bestiality and explicit sex, pandering to the illiterate. Others pointed to historical inaccuracies, and one women's studies professor dubbed the novel dreadful. As a group, male readers haven't much warmed to *The Red Tent*. One was put off by the euphemistic language and said it sounded like a cheap romance novel. Another man wrote a lengthy diatribe against the book, saying that he'd welcome a creative, feminist reading of the Dinah story—but *The Red Tent* isn't it. But despite its detractors, *The Red Tent* has attracted countless enthusiastic readers who embrace the novel as an astonishing, fresh look at women's power and sisterhood, life in biblical times, and complex family relationships that transcend time and place.

Other Books of Interest

The Red Tent draws on a rich, varied array of earlier works, from the ancient Hebrew scriptures to modern feminist novels.

FEW READERS OF *THE RED TENT* can resist comparing the novel with scripture. The first place to turn is Genesis. It's a good idea to go to a modern English rendition translated directly from the Hebrew rather than via Greek. A fine one is *The Torah: A Modern Commentary*, edited by W. Gunther Plaut (Union of American Hebrew Congregations, 1981). The most relevant passages of Genesis are chapters 29–34, along with its commentary.

There are several important feminist interpretations of the Bible, among them *The Women's Bible Commentary*, edited by Carol Newsom and Sharon Ringe. Newsome and Ringe make the case that the vengeance visited upon Shechem has less to do with Dinah's honor than with the male-dominated political realities in Canaan. Dr. Ellen Frankel's *The Five Books of Miriam* presents the world of the Pentateuch as a series of intimate conversations in the first-person voices of biblical women. Dinah, called the Wounded One, is one of the voices we hear. Also thumb through Alan Dershowitz's *The Genesis of Justice*, in which he shows us a Jacob who soundly rebukes his sons for their deeds in Shechem, but not on moral grounds. Jacob's concern is his image and his fear of retaliation from neighbors. Dershowitz reminds us that if a rape did occur, the law of the Israelites didn't punish rape with death. In this light, the vengeance of Levi and Simon is overkill—in the truest sense of the word.

Three other novels about Jacob's family are particularly enlightening. The first, Thomas Mann's *Joseph and His Brothers,* is intimidating in the manner of modern fiction translated from German. Nonetheless, it devotes a chapter to Dinah and the tragedy in Shechem, painting an intimate picture of Jacob's unruly brood.

A somewhat more accessible novel is Frederick Buechner's *Son of Laughter,* told in Jacob's voice as he relates to his grandfather Abraham the dreadful catastrophe in Shechem. Jacob views Shalem as a lad smitten by the beautiful, blue-eyed Dinah, refusing to believe that this beardless boy took Dinah by force. Further, Jacob explains the outrageous response of his sons as their own lecherous impulses are projected onto the young prince.

Deena Metzger goes even further in her novel *What Dinah Thought.* Like Diamant, Metzger casts the alleged rape as a tender romance. But in a departure from both Diamant and Buechner, Metzger filters her interpretation of Dinah through the eyes of a filmmaker visiting Israel to make a documentary on how ancient history affects modern people living on the same hallowed ground.

The Red Tent often inspires curiosity about goddess worship, and there are two good sources to consult for more information on this topic. *The Great Cosmic Mother: Rediscovering the Religion of the Earth* by Monica Sjoo and Barbara Mor claims that the first measure of time was menstrual time, from which women developed lunar calendars. *The Great Cosmic Mother* also contends that the ongoing battle over goddess worship vs. monotheism is the primary theme of Hebrew Scripture, beginning in Genesis when a male God takes over the Goddess's Garden of Immortality. Traditionalists would certainly dispute this claim.

An even better book is Patricia Monaghan's *The New Book of Goddesses and Heroines.* In alphabetical entries, it names hundreds of goddesses in world culture and the legends associated with them. Of special interest are the goddesses of the ancient Near East mentioned in *The Red Tent.* One such is Gula (Rachel's favorite), who both inflicts and heals illness.

The Red Tent also provides a thorough exploration of midwifery, but it's hardly the first book on the topic. *The Midwife* by Gay Courter doesn't delve into ancient history but instead paints an early-twentieth-century picture. The Jewish midwife of the title practices her calling from Czarist Russia to Manhattan's Lower East Side, encountering romance, intrigue, and nearly as many births as Diamant delivers in her novel.

Another excellent title is a juvenile novel by Karen Cushman about a twelfth-century orphan who becomes *The Midwife's Apprentice*. The essay in the back of the novel provides a wealth of information on the practices, herbs, and psychology of midwifery throughout history.

Finally, Diamant's six books preceding *The Red Tent* are full of bits of interesting information that bear relevance to her novel. These previous books are nonfiction handbooks on contemporary Jewish practice and custom, from birth to death. Diamant's follow-up to *The Red Tent*, her novel *Good Harbor*, is also about the power of female friendship and the importance of women sharing their personal stories. This second novel explores Jewish identity issues, along with the life-and-death concerns that trouble two friends in a Massachusetts seaside town. *Good Harbor* is smaller in scope and contemporary in flavor, so it's a departure from *The Red Tent*—as will be Diamant's next novel, which she's revealed will have a nineteenth-century setting.